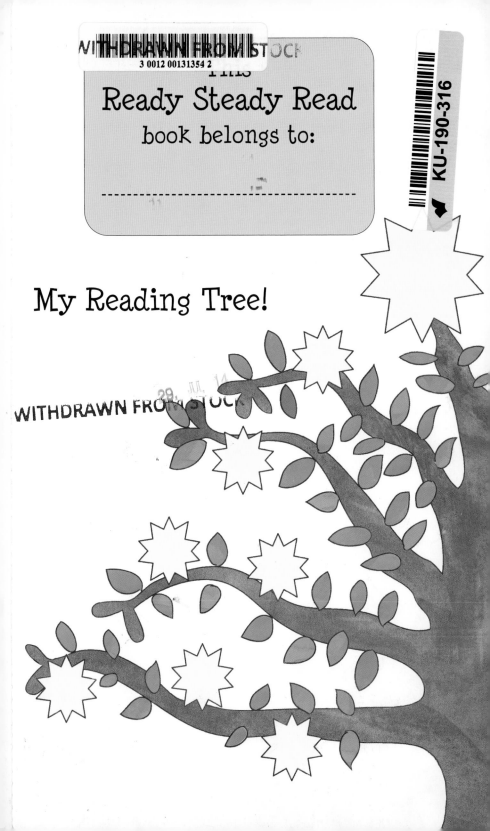

WITHDRAWN FROM STOCK

3 0012 00131354 2

WITHDRAWN FROM STOCK

KU-190-316

This

Ready Steady Read
book belongs to:

My Reading Tree!

For Bob and Sue
~ N W

LITTLE TIGER PRESS
An imprint of Magi Publications
1 The Coda Centre, 189 Munster Road, London SW6 6AW
www.littletigerpress.com

First published in Great Britain 2005
This edition published 2009

Text and illustrations copyright © Nick Ward 2005
Nick Ward has asserted his right to be identified as the author and illustrator
of this work under the Copyright, Designs and Patents Act, 1988

All rights reserved • ISBN 978-1-84506-876-9

Printed in China

2 4 6 8 10 9 7 5 3 1

The
BIGGEST
BADDEST
WOLF

Nick
Ward

Limerick
County Library
00638256

LITTLE TIGER PRESS
London

"I am the GREATEST!" howled Harum Scarum, admiring himself in the mirror as he brushed his fangs. "I am the biggest, baddest, hairiest, scariest wolf in the city!"

Limerick
County Library

Harum Scarum looked at his watch. "Time for some fun," he said.

Harum Scarum's idea of fun was to scare people. Well, he was the biggest, baddest, hairiest, scariest wolf in the city!

"Have I got everything?" he wondered, patting his pockets. "Money, sweets, Teddy . . . Oops, where's my teddy?"

Nobody knew that Harum Scarum had a teddy, and that he couldn't go anywhere without him.

"Ah! There you are!" he sighed, giving Teddy a big, wet, wolfy kiss.

He put Teddy in his back pocket and went off happily.

First stop was the park where Harum Scarum had some fun scaring all the little children playing on the swings.

"Run, little children, run, or I'll eat you up!"

he howled.

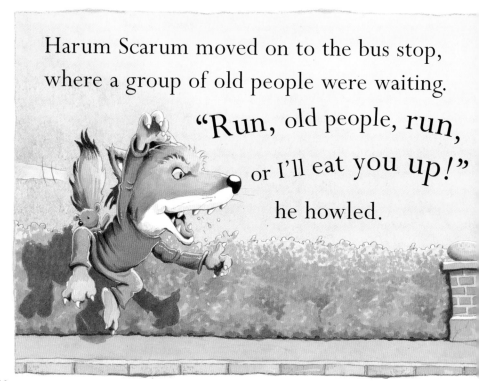

Harum Scarum moved on to the bus stop, where a group of old people were waiting.

"Run, old people, run, or I'll eat you up!"

he howled.

"Eeek!" they screamed and rushed away.
"I am the biggest, baddest, hairiest,
scariest wolf in the city!" he called
after them.

"Eeek!" they screamed,
and tottered all the way home.
"I am the biggest, baddest, hairiest,
scariest wolf in the city!" he called
after them.

For the rest of the day Harum Scarum
worked very hard
at scaring
anyone
he could.

He startled a skateboarder . . .

He petrified
a builder . . .

And he made a street juggler jump.
"This is fantastic fun,"
he cried.

By the time he got home, he was so tired he decided to go straight to bed. And that's when he discovered . . . he'd lost his teddy!

"Oh no!" he said, frantically searching his room. He looked here and there . . . but he couldn't find Teddy anywhere.

Harum Scarum crawled sadly
into bed. He tossed and turned,
but he couldn't get to sleep
without his teddy to cuddle.

The next morning Harum Scarum was
a nervous wreck. "I must find my teddy,"
he wailed, and hurried outside without
even brushing his fangs. He paced the
streets. He searched in every alleyway.

He looked high . . .

and low . . .

But Teddy was nowhere to be seen.

Finally he arrived at the bus stop. "Excuse me, have you seen a teddy?" he asked the old people.

But as soon as they saw him they tottered off home shouting, "Help, it's the biggest, baddest, hairiest, scariest wolf in the city!"

Harum Scarum went to the park.
"Excuse me . . ." he began, but
the little children all rushed off
shouting, "Help, it's the biggest,
baddest, hairiest, scariest wolf
in the city!"

Harum Scarum sighed, and a tear rolled down his cheek. But just then he noticed one little boy left playing on his own. And he was playing with . . . Harum Scarum's teddy!

"My teddy!" gasped Harum Scarum.

"*My* teddy!" said the little boy. "Finders keepers."

"Please give him back," Harum Scarum whimpered. "I'm the biggest, baddest, hairiest, scariest wolf in the city."

"You don't look so scary to me,"
said the little boy.

"Please!" cried Harum Scarum.
"I'd do anything to get Teddy back."

"Do you promise to do exactly
what you're told from now on?"
smiled the little boy.

"Of course," he said.

The very next morning, after a good night's sleep, Harum Scarum brushed his fangs and patted his pockets. Whistling happily, he left home and went straight to the park.

"Hurry up," cried the little children. "We're on the swings! Come and push us."

"Coming," smiled Harum Scarum.
He trotted up to the children . . .

Limerick
County Library
00638256

21

"Run, little children, run,
or I'll eat you up!"

"Eeek!" cried the children,
rushing off. "You promised . . ."
    "Well, what did you expect?"
chuckled Harum Scarum,
hugging his teddy. "You should
never trust the biggest, baddest,
hairiest, scariest wolf in the city!"